I'm going to read

I'm Going To **READ**!

These levels are meant only as guides;
you and your child can best choose a book that's right.

Level 1: Kindergarten–Grade 1 . . . Ages 4–6
- word bank to highlight new words
- consistent placement of text to promote readability
- easy words and phrases
- simple sentences build to make simple stories
- art and design help new readers decode text

Level 2: Grade 1 . . . Ages 6–7
- word bank to highlight new words
- rhyming texts introduced
- more difficult words, but vocabulary is still limited
- longer sentences and longer stories
- designed for easy readability

Level 3: Grade 2 . . . Ages 7–8
- richer vocabulary of up to 200 different words
- varied sentence structure
- high-interest stories with longer plots
- designed to promote independent reading

Level 4: Grades 3 and up . . . Ages 8 and up
- richer vocabulary of more than 300 different words
- short chapters, multiple stories, or poems
- more complex plots for the newly independent reade
- emphasis on reading for meaning

Note to Parents

What a great sense of achievement it is when you can accomplish a goal. With the **I'm Going To Read** series, goals are established when you pick up a book. This series was developed to grow with the new reader. The vocabulary grows quantifiably from 50 different words at level one, to 100 different words at level two, to 200 different words at level three, and to 300 different words at level four.

Ways to Use the Word Bank

- Read along with your child and help him or her sound out the words in the word bank.

- Have your child find the word in the word bank as you read it aloud.

- Ask your child to find the correct word in the word bank to match the artwork.

- Review the words in the word bank before reading the story and ask your child to read the story to you.

Related Word Bank Activities

- Create mini-flash cards in your handwriting (this provides yet another opportunity for the reader to be able to identify words, regardless of what the type looks like). Ask your child to pick a word to start a sentence. Take turns placing the flash cards in a row until you make a sentence.

- Think of a sentence and then place the mini-flash cards on a table out of order. Ask your child to rearrange the mini-flash cards until the sentence makes sense.

- Make up riddles about words in the story and have your child find the appropriate mini-flash card. For example, "It's red and it bounces. What is it?" Your child will find the mini-flash card for *ball*. Or use a rhyming word, "I'm thinking of a word that rhymes with *sing*. What is it?"

- Choose one of the mini-flash cards and ask your child to find the same word in the text of the story.

- Create a second set of mini-flash cards and play concentration, trying to match the pairs of words.

LEVEL 1

Library of Congress Cataloging-in-Publication Data Available

4 6 8 10 9 7 5 3

Published by Sterling Publishing Co., Inc.
387 Park Avenue South, New York, NY 10016
Text copyright © 2005 by Harriet Ziefert Inc.
Illustrations copyright © 2005 by Laura Rader
Distributed in Canada by Sterling Publishing
c/o Canadian Manda Group, 165 Dufferin Street
Toronto, Ontario, Canada M6K 3H6
Distributed in Great Britain and Europe by Chris Lloyd at Orca Book
Services, Stanley House, Fleets Lane, Poole BH15 3AJ, England
Distributed in Australia by Capricorn Link (Australia) Pty. Ltd.
P.O. Box 704, Windsor, NSW 2756, Australia

Printed in China
Sterling ISBN 1-4027-2093-9

I Hate Boots!

Pictures by Laura Rader

Sterling Publishing Co., Inc.
New York

"Can I play outside?"
asked Molly.

"Yes, if you wear your snowsuit,"
said her mother.

"Here are your boots,"
said Molly's mother.

"You need boots!"

"I hate boots!"
said Molly.

"Here is your hat,"
said Molly's mother.

"You need a hat,"
said Molly's mother.

"I hate hats!"
said Molly.

"Here is your scarf,"
said Molly's mother.

"You need a scarf!"

"I hate scarves!"

"Here are your mittens,"
said Molly's mother.

"You need mittens!"

"Now you can go outside,"
said Molly's mother.

"I hate snowsuits!"
said Molly.

Molly went outside to play.

She made a snowman.

"Snowman, you need a scarf.
You need mittens."

"Snowman, I need my hat,"
said Molly.

"I need my mittens.
I need my scarf."

"I'm not cold now," said Molly.
"I'm warm!"